KU-515-180

Family Storybook Library

Say What You Mean and Do What You Say

Stories About Honesty and Integrity

BOOK FOUR

Copyright © 2000 by Disney Enterprises, Inc.

All rights reserved. No part of this book may be reproduced or
transmitted in any form or by any means, electronic or mechanical,
including photocopying, recording, or by any information storage
and retrieval system, without written permission from the publisher.
For information address Disney Press,
114 Fifth Avenue, New York, New York 10011-5690.

First Edition
1 3 5 7 9 10 8 6 4 2

ISBN: 0-7868-5869-9

Say What You Mean and Do What You Say

Stories About Honesty and Integrity

Introduction

Children need to feel that the world is a fair and just place. This helps them to find a sense of order in their own lives. Although we know that the world is not always just or fair, we need to encourage them to apply these values to their everyday actions. We must urge them to treat others as they would hope to be treated, with respect and without prejudice.

In "A Fair Fight," Peter Pan decides to stick to his principles and fight fairly with Captain Hook, no matter what the consequences. Pinocchio learns, in "A Nose for Mischief," that all dishonesty will be revealed in due time.

A Fair Fight

from *Peter Pan*

⸺∞⸺

To earn people's trust:
Say what you mean and do what you say.

In a pirate ship anchored near the island of Never Land, Captain Hook faced his greatest enemy, Peter Pan. The Captain was furious at Peter for having rescued Wendy, her brothers, and the Lost Boys.

After safely installing the children in the crow's nest, Peter flew down to the yardarm.

"Fly! Fly! You coward!" cried Hook.

"Coward?" said Peter. "Me?"

Hook started to climb the rigging. "You wouldn't dare fight old Hook man to man," the Captain taunted. "You'd fly away like a cowardly sparrow."

"Nobody calls me a coward!"

Peter replied. "I'll fight you man to man, with one hand tied behind my back!"

Hook joined Peter on the yardarm and locked blades with him. As they stood face-to-face, dagger to sword, Hook said mischievously, "You won't fly?"

Wendy called down from the crow's nest. "Don't do it, Peter! It's a trick."

"I give my word," said Peter.

Hook shouted, "Then let's have at it!"

The duel began. Hook pushed Peter off the yardarm, but Peter grabbed the edge just in time. Peter pulled himself back onto the yardarm, and the fight continued.

As Peter struggled to maintain his balance, Hook knocked the dagger out of Peter's hand. The dagger splashed into the water below. Hook snarled, "Insolent youth—prepare to die!"

"Fly!" Wendy and the boys cried. "Please, Peter, fly!"

"No!" Peter shouted up to them. "I gave my word."

Carefully, Peter felt his way backward

along the yardarm. Any second now, he could tumble into the sea or be pierced by the Captain's sword.

As Hook drew back his weapon one last time, Peter looked up and saw a black pirate flag fluttering above the yardarm. Peter jumped up, grabbed the flag, and pulled it down over the Captain's head. While Hook thrashed beneath the banner, Peter seized the captain's sword.

"You're mine, Hook," said Peter triumphantly.

Hook untangled himself from the cloth. He looked down at the sea and saw the crocodile waiting for him. "You wouldn't do old Hook in, now would you, lad?" he said, trembling. "I'll go away forever. I'll do anything you say!"

"All right," Peter said good-humoredly. "Say you're a codfish."

Hook shuddered, horrified.

"Say it!" Peter demanded.

Hook gulped, then said meekly, "I'm a . . . codfish."

"Louder!" Peter demanded.

"I'm a codfish!" Hook screamed. Above him, the boys in the crow's nest began to chant, "Hook is a codfish! Hook is a codfish!"

The Captain was thoroughly humiliated. That blasted Peter Pan had kept his word . . . and beat him!

A Nose for Mischief

from *Pinocchio*

Lies told to avoid trouble usually make more.

O n his way to school one day, the little
wooden boy, Pinocchio, met two shady
characters who convinced him to join
a marionette show. Pinocchio went onstage
and thrilled the audience by dancing without
strings.

That night, Pinocchio couldn't wait to get
home to tell his father, the woodcarver
Geppetto, about his performance.

"Home?" said Stromboli the puppeteer,
sneering. "Very funny."

He grabbed Pinocchio and tossed him into

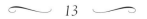

a birdcage. Then he snapped the padlock
shut and left Pinocchio alone in the back of
the wagon.

Soon Jiminy Cricket caught up with the
wagon and hopped in back. "I should have kept
my eye on you," said Jiminy, who had been

appointed by
the Blue Fairy
to be Pinocchio's
conscience.

Pinocchio
and Jiminy
looked out the
back of the
wagon at the
starlit sky. One
star blazed and
began spinning
toward the wagon. The whirling starlight
settled in front of Pinocchio's cage, and the
Blue Fairy appeared.

"Why, Pinocchio," she said. "Why didn't
you go to school?"

"Well, you see," he replied slowly,

"I was going to school until I met somebody. . . ."

"Met somebody?" said the Blue Fairy.

"Right," continued Pinocchio. "Two big monsters—with big green eyes!"

"Weren't you afraid?" asked the Blue Fairy.

"No, ma'am," said Pinocchio firmly. "But they tied me in a big sack!"

"You don't say . . ." mused the Blue Fairy.

Pinocchio told one lie after another, and each time he lied, his wooden nose grew. It grew and grew, until it poked out of the cage and sprouted leaves. Among the leaves was a bird's nest, with a family of birds!

"Look! My nose!" cried Pinocchio. "What's happening to it?"

"Perhaps you haven't been telling the truth, Pinocchio," said the Blue Fairy. "You see, a lie keeps growing until it's as plain as the nose on your face."

Pinocchio blurted, "I'll never lie again. Honest, I won't!"

"I'll forgive you this once," said the Blue

Fairy. "But this is the last time I can help you. Remember, a boy who won't be good might just as well be made of wood."

The Blue Fairy tapped Pinocchio on his nose with her magic wand, then vanished.

Pinocchio's nose returned to normal, and the lock on the cage magically opened. Pinocchio was free to pursue

his dream of becoming a real boy.
It was a dream that would come true—
as long as he remained truthful.